This is

MR. BUMBA PLANTS A GARDEN

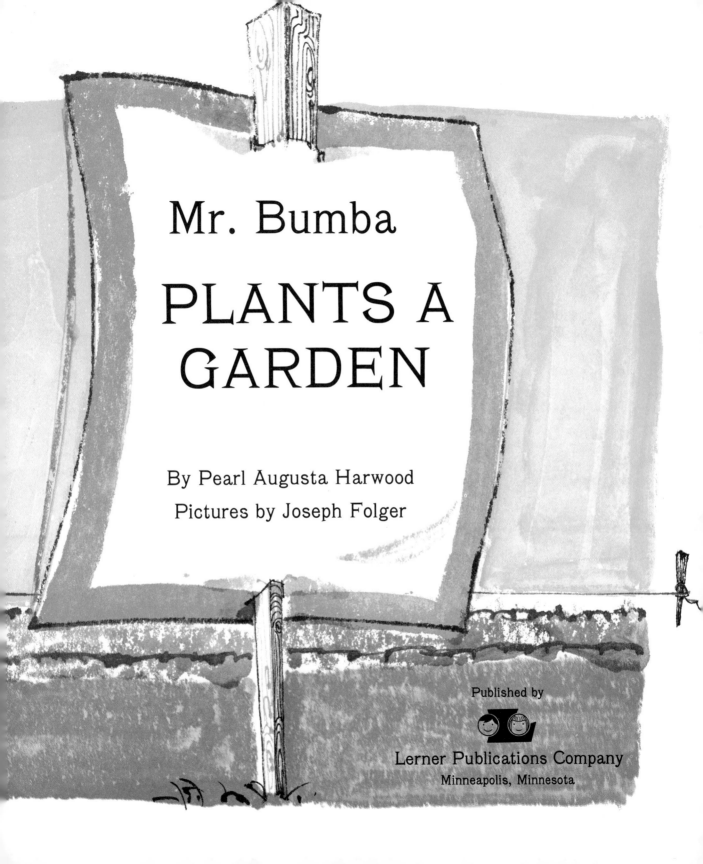

Mr. Bumba

PLANTS A
GARDEN

By Pearl Augusta Harwood
Pictures by Joseph Folger

Published by

Lerner Publications Company
Minneapolis, Minnesota

The type used
in this book is
MR. BUMBA TEXT
set in 16 point.

International Standard Book Number: 0-8225-0102-3
Library of Congress Catalog Card Number: 64-19771

Sixth Printing 1971

Mr. A. C. Bumba lived in his Aunt Mary's house.

His Aunt Mary had gone to live with her friend in another city.

Mr. Bumba lived all alone, but his two neighbors, Jane and Bill visited him every day.

Jane lived on one side of him and Bill lived
on the other.

They came through gates in the
high wooden fence.

The fence on Mr. Bumba's side was full of pictures.

Mr. Bumba was always painting pictures, for that was his work.

"Painting pictures is your work," said Jane one day, "but what do you do when you play?"

"Play?" said Mr. Bumba. "Should I play?"

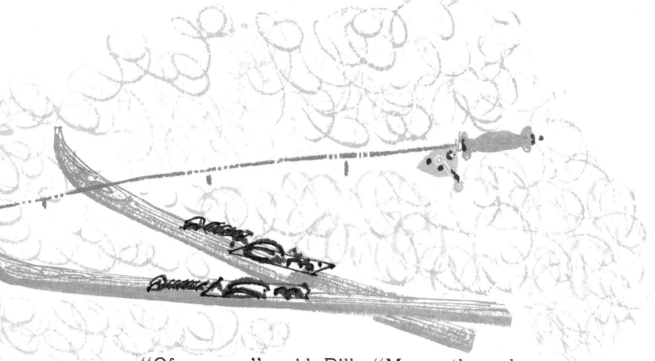

"Of course," said Bill. "My mother plays bridge. My father plays golf."

"And we play all sorts of things," said Jane.

Mr. Bumba scratched his head.

"I think," said he, "that I would like to play with a garden."

Jane and Bill looked around Mr. Bumba's backyard.

"There isn't any garden here," said Jane. "Only grass."

"There <u>could</u> be a garden," said Bill. "If you took out some of the grass."

"That is what I could do," said Mr. Bumba.

So they got some spades and took out the grass from part of the backyard. It took a good bit of time, but it was fun.

Mr. Bumba shook the dirt from the roots of the grass. He saved the grass in a pile.

"Why do you do that?" asked Jane.

"I will let it rot," said Mr. Bumba. "After it rots, I will put it in the ground to make the garden grow better."

"I hope you will have pretty flowers in your garden," said Jane.

"I hope you will have vegetables," said Bill. "Vegetables are useful. You can eat them."

"Flowers are pretty," said Jane. "You can look at them, and smell them, too."

"Vegetables are better," said Bill. He frowned at Jane.

"Flowers are better," said Jane. She frowned too, and stamped her foot.

"Vegetables!"

"Flowers!"

"Vegetables!"

"Flowers!" They were shouting at each other.

Mr. Bumba scratched his head.

"Hold on!" he said. "I feel an idea coming.
It's almost here."

"What is it?" said Jane and Bill.

"Come over tomorrow, and you will see,"
said Mr. Bumba.

The next morning Mr. Bumba did not work at painting pictures. He went shopping.

First he put food in his shopping cart. Then he went to the seed stand.

There were envelopes of many kinds. Each envelope had a picture of a plant. The picture showed what kind of plants would grow from the seeds inside.

Mr. Bumba bought lettuce seeds.

He bought
beet seeds,
carrot seeds,

and radish seeds.
These were all vegetables.

Then he bought aster seeds, poppy seeds,

marigold seeds and

zinnia seeds.

These were all flowers.

He planted almost all the seeds, in his garden, himself. But he saved some seeds for Bill and Jane to plant.

"What can I plant?" asked Jane, when she came over.

"You can plant these poppy seeds," said Mr. Bumba. "Plant them right along this line."

"That is really four lines," said Jane. "And it looks like the letter "E".

"So it does," said Bill. "Now what can I plant?"

"You can plant these radish seeds," said Mr. Bumba. "Plant them right along this line."

"This is really two lines," said Bill. "And it looks like the letter "L".

"So it does," said Jane.

"Mr. Bumba has vegetables," said Bill. "He has radishes."

"He has flowers, too." said Jane. "He has poppies."

So they were both happy.

They watched for all the seeds to come up. It took a long time. Some seeds came up before others.

Jane and Bill helped water Mr. Bumba's garden.

They did not pull weeds. They were not sure which were weeds and which were the plants they wanted.

Mr. Bumba did know, and he pulled the weeds.

After a few weeks, there was a rain. It rained for two days. Then the sun came out.

Jane and Bill came over to Mr. Bumba's yard. They looked at the garden.

They smiled very wide smiles, and Mr. Bumba smiled too.

The seeds were all up. But there were no blossoms yet.

All the flower seeds made letters on the ground.

The vegetables seeds made letters, too.

The aster plants made the letter "J".

The zinnia plants made the letter "A".

The marigold plants made the letter "N".

The poppy plants made the letter "E".

The lettuce plants made the letter "B".

The beet plants made the letter "I".

The carrot plants made the letter "L".

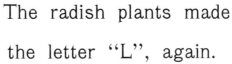

The radish plants made
the letter "L", again.

The whole garden looked like this.

"What a surprise!" said Bill.

"How pretty!" said Jane.

And a few weeks later, when the flowers
blossomed, it was prettier still.

The vegetables did not blossom, but they were very good to eat. Mr. Bumba gave Jane and Bill some to take home.

He gave them some flowers, too.

And Bill liked the flowers just as much as Jane did.

And Jane liked the vegetables just as much as Bill did.

Mr. Bumba liked everything anyway.

He thought it was great fun to play in a garden.